My Weirder School #5

Ms. Beard Is Weird!

Dan Gutman

Pictures by
Jim Paillot

HARPER

An Imprint of HarperCollins Publishers

To Blake and Colby Wiener

My Weirder School #5: Ms. Beard Is Weird!

Text copyright © 2012 by Dan Gutman

Illustrations copyright © 2012 by Jim Paillot

Library of Congress Cataloging-in-Publication Data is available.

ISBN 978-0-06-204210-1 (lib. bdg.) — ISBN 978-0-06-204209-5 (pbk.)

Typography by Kate Engbring

12 13 14 15 16   CG/BR   10 9 8 7 6 5 4 3

❖

First Edition

Contents

Hooray for Mr. Klutz!

My name is A.J. and I hate it when a helicopter lands on my head.

Okay, so a helicopter never *really* landed on my head. But I'm pretty sure that if a helicopter ever *did* land on my head, I would hate it. Wouldn't you?

My teacher is Mr. Granite, who is from

another planet. He's been pretty angry lately. Every time he tries to teach us anything, an announcement comes over the loudspeaker telling us to go to an assembly. Mr. Granite got so mad that he yanked the loudspeaker out of the wall!

"Okay, today we're going to talk about the Civil War," Mr. Granite told us. "Turn to page twenty-three in your—"

He didn't get the chance to finish his sentence, because you'll never believe who poked her head into the door at that moment.

Nobody! It would hurt if you poked your head into a door. Why would anybody want to do a dumb thing like that?

But you'll never believe who poked her head into the *doorway*.

It was Mrs. Patty, the school secretary!

"I've been trying to reach you," she told Mr. Granite. "Who yanked your loud-speaker out of the wall? Everyone has to report to the all-purpose room for a

surprise assembly."

"Not *again*!" yelled Mr. Granite.

Surprise assemblies are fun, because you never know what's going to happen. That's why they're called *surprise* assemblies.

We had to walk a million hundred miles to the all-purpose room. I don't know why they call it an all-purpose room, because we can't use it for *all* purposes. I mean, you can't use it to fly into outer space. So why is it called the all-purpose room?

Anyway, we had to sit boy-girl-boy-girl to make sure we wouldn't sit next to anybody we liked. I had to sit between annoying Andrea and her crybaby friend, Emily. Ugh, disgusting! I made sure not to let my elbows touch theirs.

Mr. Klutz, our principal, was up on the stage. He has no hair at all.*

"Great news, everyone!" Mr. Klutz told us. "Our budget problems are solved. I'm happy to report that we can buy new computers and supplies. We can bring back the art and music programs. We can hire all the teachers who were fired. We can turn on the water fountains again and put toilet paper back in the bathrooms."

"Hooray for Mr. Klutz!" Everybody was whistling and cheering and shouting.

"Where did you get the money to do all

_____

*He must save a lot of money on shampoo and hair dryers and stuff.

those things?" asked our librarian, Mrs. Roopy. "Did you get a grant?"

"No," said Mr. Klutz.

"Are taxes going up?" asked the school nurse, Mrs. Cooney.

"No," said Mr. Klutz.

"Are we going to have a fund-raiser?" asked Dr. Brad, the school counselor.

"No," said Mr. Klutz. "The

money is coming from the famous TV producer Ms. Beard. She's making a new reality show, and she's going to shoot it right here! It is going to be called *The Real Teachers of Ella Mentry School*."

"EEEEEEEEEKKKK!"

All the teachers were freaking out.

"We're going to be on TV!" screamed our speech teacher, Ms. Laney.

"We're going to be famous!" screamed our vice principal, Mrs. Jafee.

"How does my hair look?" screamed our computer teacher, Mrs. Yonkers.

"What am I going to wear?" screamed our Spanish teacher, Miss Holly. "I have nothing to wear!"

Teachers are weird.

Chickie Baby

Over the weekend my parents had to sign a contract that I brought home in my backpack. The contract said they couldn't sue anybody if I fell into a well, or got eaten by a lion or run over by a train, or if a helicopter fell on my head during the filming of *The Real Teachers of Ella Mentry School*.

When I got to school on Monday morning, everybody was out front, dressed up in their nicest clothes. I had to wear a tie. Ugh. It looked like we were all going to a wedding or a funeral. We had to wear badges, too, so people watching on TV would know our names.

The teachers were running around warning us to be on our best behavior for Ms. Beard. She's a big celebrity, and she was coming all the way from Hollywood. The girls were giggling and talking nervously to each other.

"My mom took me to the beauty parlor yesterday," said Andrea.

"It looks like she took you to the *ugly* parlor," I told Andrea.

"Oh, snap!" said Ryan, who will eat anything, even stuff that isn't food.

Andrea stuck out her tongue at me.

"My mom took me for a pedicure," said Emily.

"What's a pedicure?" asked Michael, who never ties his shoes.

"That's when they soak your feet and paint your toenails," Emily told us.

"Do you think they're gonna make a TV show about your toenails?" asked Neil, who we call the nude kid even though he wears clothes.

"Boys are mean!" said Emily.

"Do you think this dress makes me look fat?" Andrea asked the other girls.

"Yes," I told her.

"I wasn't asking *you*, *Arlo*!"

Andrea calls me by my real name because she knows I don't like it. I wanted to make fun of her some more, but at that moment the most amazing thing in the history of the world happened. A black limousine pulled up at the other side of the playground. It was really long, like somebody took two regular-sized cars and stuck them together. The windows were tinted, so we couldn't see inside.

"Ms. Beard is here!" yelled Alexia, who is a girl but pretty cool anyway.

"Ms. Beard is here!" yelled Ryan.

"Ms. Beard is here!" yelled Michael.

In case you were wondering, everybody was yelling that Ms. Beard was here.

But actually, Ms. Beard *wasn't* here. Not yet anyway.

A bunch of guys got out of the limo. They were carrying cameras and lights and stuff.

A few seconds later, a helicopter came down from the sky and landed on the playground near the limo. A lady got out.

"It's Ms. Beard!" shouted Mr. Klutz.

Ms. Beard climbed down from the helicopter and got into the limo. Then the limo drove about ten yards to where we were all waiting. I guess Ms. Beard doesn't like to walk.

"Remember," shouted Mr. Klutz, "we want to show Ms. Beard what terrific students we have at Ella Mentry School. Everybody be on your best behavior."

"I'm *always* on my best behavior," said Andrea.

What is her problem?

Ms. Beard got out of the limo and looked around.

"Welcome to our school," Mr. Klutz told her. "I'm sure you'll find our children—"

He didn't get the chance to finish his sentence, because Ms. Beard wasn't paying attention.

"Fabulous, Chickie Baby!" she said. "I love children! They're like grown-ups, only shorter."

"We should probably talk about—" said Mr. Klutz.

"Sure, let's do lunch, Chickie Baby," said Ms. Beard.

"Uh, I just did breakfast," said Mr. Klutz. "And my name isn't Chickie Baby. It's Mr. Klutz."

"Not *now*, Chickie Baby," said Ms. Beard. "Let's do lunch at *lunchtime,* sweetie. Have your girl call my girl. We'll take a meeting."

She talks funny.

The big guys started setting up lights, cameras, and microphones everywhere. Ms. Beard walked around looking us over like a general inspecting the troops.

"Oh, this is going to be *fabulous*!" she said. "It will be the first reality show that

15

takes place in a school. The ratings are going to go through the roof!"

"Are we going to be famous like that Snookie lady?" asked Andrea.

"That depends on what happens, baby,"* said Ms. Beard. "This is reality TV. We don't use scripts. Nobody has any lines. It's all about reality. We'll just have to see what happens."

"When does the show begin?" asked Neil the nude kid.

"Right now, baby!" Ms. Beard said, clapping her hands together.

Somebody gave her a big megaphone, and she shouted into it, "Quiet on the set!

---

*Ms. Beard calls everybody "baby." I wonder what she calls *real* babies.

16

We're shooting *The Real Teachers of Ella Mentry School*! Lights! Camera! ACTION!"

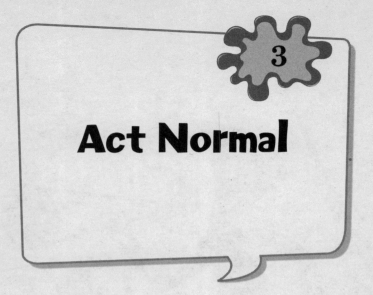

Act Normal

Mr. Klutz reminded us again to be on our best behavior. The morning bell rang, and we rushed up the steps and down the hall to our classroom. It was weird with those guys sticking cameras in our faces.

"How do I look?" Mr. Granite whispered to us as we walked down the hall. "I'm a little nervous. I've never been on TV before."

"You look like a real TV star, Mr. Granite!" said Andrea.

What a brownnoser.

Finally, we got to class and took our seats. There were four cameras and cameramen and long sticks with microphones hanging all over the place. Ms. Beard sat on a chair in the back of the room. I guess she takes her chair with her everywhere, because it had her name on the back of it.

"Okay, just pretend I'm not here," Ms. Beard told Mr. Granite. "Act like it's any other day at school. ACTION!"

"Uh . . . good morning, boys and girls,"

said Mr. Granite. "Today we're going to . . . uh . . . talk about . . . uh . . . the Civil War. Turn to page . . . uh . . . twenty-three in your books. . . ."

We all turned to page twenty-three.

"The Civil War," Mr. Granite continued, "um . . . uh . . . it wasn't very . . . um . . . civil at all. Ha-ha. Just a little joke there. Ummmm, I mean . . . can I do that over again, Ms. Beard? I messed up."

Ms. Beard jumped up and put her arm around his shoulder.

"Granite, baby, you just gotta *relax*," she said. "Just be yourself. Act normal. Okay? Let's try it again."

Ms. Beard went back to her chair and yelled "ACTION!" again.

"The Civil War," said Mr. Granite, ". . . uh . . . ummm, it reminds me of a story my grandmother told me.

Blah blah blah blah blah blah blah blah blah blah blah blah blah blah blah blah."

Mr. Granite started telling a story about his grandmother. It went on forever. I thought I was gonna die. It's hard to sit still without fidgeting. But I kept my feet on the floor and my hands folded on my desk. I didn't want Mr. Granite to call on me, so I made sure not to look at him. That's the first rule of being a kid.

"Blah blah blah blah blah blah blah blah blah blah blah blah . . . ," droned Mr. Granite.

Suddenly, Andrea raised her hand.

"Yes, Andrea?"

"Is it true that the Civil War started in

1861 when eleven Southern states decided to leave the United States and form their own country called the Confederate States of America?"

Ugh. I hate her.

"That's absolutely right!" said Mr. Granite, beaming at Andrea. "I can see you've been studying."

"I always try my hardest," Andrea said. Then she made a big smile right into the camera.

Why can't a truckload of cameras fall on her head?

"Beautiful! Cut!" said Ms. Beard. "Okay, guys. Let's move to the next class."

The cameramen started picking up their equipment.

"When will we be on TV?" asked Andrea.

"Tonight, baby," Ms. Beard replied.

"EEEEEEEEEEK! We're gonna be on TV *tonight*!"

Everybody was freaking out.

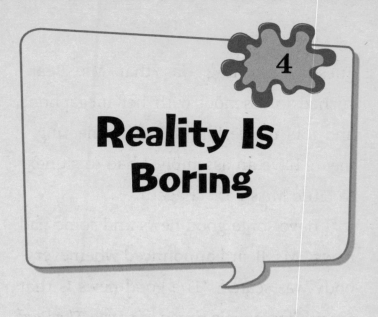

Reality Is Boring

My parents let me stay up late on Monday to watch *The Real Teachers of Ella Mentry School*. It was cool to see us all on TV, even if I had to look at Andrea's big face hogging the screen the whole time.

The first thing that happened on

Tuesday morning was that Ms. Beard rushed into school with her megaphone and told us we had to take a meeting. I mean, have an assembly. I had to sit next to Little Miss Perfect again.

"I have some good news and some bad news," Ms. Beard announced when everybody was seated. "The good news is that ten million people tuned in to see *The Real Teachers of Ella Mentry School* last night."

"WOW," we all said, which is "MOM" upside down.

"What's the bad news?" asked Mr. Klutz.

"The bad news is that nine million of them turned the show off after five minutes," said Ms. Beard.

"What?" we all asked. "Why?"

"Because it was *boring,* that's why!" Ms. Beard told us. "Nobody wants to watch polite, well-behaved kids being taught by excellent teachers. They can see that at their *own* school."

"I thought the show was supposed to be *real,*" said Mrs. Jafee. "Isn't that why they call it a *reality* show?"

"Let me tell you a little secret," said Ms. Beard. "Reality is boring. People don't want to watch reality. They want to be *amazed*. We've got to show them something they've never seen before. We've got to blow their minds!"

"I thought you told us to act normal,"

said Mr. Granite.

"Look," said Ms. Beard. "Normal is boring. If you folks can't spice things up, *The Real Teachers of Ella Mentry School* is going to be canceled."

"Canceled!?" Mr. Klutz looked all panicked. "Does that mean we won't get the money you promised?"

"That's right, Chickie Baby."

"Stop calling me Chickie Baby!" said Mr. Klutz.

"If the show is canceled, there goes the music and art programs again," moaned Ms. Hannah, our art teacher.

"There goes the water fountains," moaned Mrs. Patty.

"There goes the toilet paper," moaned

Miss Lazar, our custodian.

"Hey, lighten up!" Ms. Beard said. "I know how we can make *The Real Teachers of Ella Mentry School* into a hit. I have a plan. Trust me. Show business is in my blood."*

"What's the plan?" Mr. Klutz asked. "We need to save the show."

"People like winners and losers," Ms. Beard said as she got out a large shopping bag. "So here's what I'm going to do. I'm going to divide a group of teachers into two teams. One team will wear hats with antlers on them. They will be called the Mooseketeers. The other team will wear these hot dog hats, and they will be the

---

*She should go to the doctor.

29

Hot Dog Heads."

Ms. Beard pulled a bunch of hats out of her bag.

"I'm not wearing a silly hat," announced Mr. Loring, our music teacher.

"Then you can't be on the show," said Ms. Beard.

"Where's my silly hat?" asked Mr. Loring.

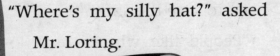

"Okay!" said Ms. Beard. "When I call your name, come up on the stage. The Mooseketeers are . . . Ms. Leakey, Ms. Hannah, Mr. Loring, Mr. Macky, Miss Holly, and Mrs. Yonkers. Come on down!"

We all cheered as the Mooseketeers ran up on the stage and high-fived each other.

"The Hot Dog Heads are . . . Mrs. Roopy, Miss Small, Mr. Docker, Mr. Granite, Ms. Coco, and Miss Laney. Come on down!"

The Hot Dog Heads fist-bumped each other as they ran up on the stage. They all put on their silly hats. The cameramen filmed everything.

"The Mooseketeers stink!" shouted Miss Laney.

"The Hot Dog Heads suck eggs!"

shouted Miss Holly.

"I'm glad to see you teachers are getting into the spirit of the competition," said Ms. Beard.

"It's not nice to call people names," Andrea said to me. "They're not setting a good example for children."

"Can you possibly be more boring?" I told Andrea.

Ms. Beard clapped her hands to get everyone's attention.

"Over the next few days," she said, "the Mooseketeers and the Hot Dog Heads will compete in a series of events. A panel of judges will help decide who is the winner, and people at home will be able to vote too."

That's when Little Miss Perfect got up to ask a question.

"Excuse me," Andrea said, "but what does this have to do with education? Shouldn't we be learning things in school?"

"Booooooooo!"

"Sit down!"

Everybody was hooting at Andrea, even some of the teachers. Nah-nah-nah boo-boo on her. It was the greatest moment of my life.

"Don't worry," Ms. Beard said. "You're going to be learning plenty. And here's the best part. One by one, the teachers will be eliminated until we're left with just one winner. That teacher will get the grand prize: a fabulous, all-expenses-paid

vacation to anywhere in the world and a year's supply of pork sausages!"

"I *love* pork sausages!" said Ms. Leakey.

"That reminds me," Ms. Beard said as she looked into one of the cameras. "Folks, do you like pork sausages? I sure do. And when I want a pork sausage, I reach for Porky's pork sausages. They're the best pork sausages in the world, made with the finest pork and no artificial ingredients. So when you want a pork sausage, reach for Porky's. Okay, let the games begin!"

Ella Mentry Idol

Mr. Klutz sent us to lunch so the teachers could get ready. When we got back to the all-purpose room, the stage was decorated with lots of lights and a big sign . . .

ELLA MENTRY IDOL!

Ms. Beard came out onstage, followed by the Mooseketeers and the Hot Dog Heads. We all yelled and screamed, but we quieted down when Mr. Klutz made a peace sign, which means "shut up."

"Welcome to Ella Mentry Idol!" said Ms. Beard. "Today we're going to see how well these twelve teachers can sing! Sadly, one of them will be eliminated."

"Awwwwwwwwww."

"Each of the teachers will sing a song," said Ms. Beard. "Then we'll open up the phone lines so viewers can vote for their favorite. The teacher who gets the fewest votes will be eliminated. Is everyone excited?"

"Yeah!" we all screamed.

"Now let's meet our judges!" said Ms. Beard.

She picked up a jar filled with slips of

paper. She shook it up and then picked out three of them.

"Our judges will be . . . Ryan, Andrea, and A.J.! Come on down!"

"That's *me*!" Andrea shrieked, jumping up and down.

We went running up to the stage and sat at the table there.

"May I ask a question?" said Andrea. "What does a singing competition have to do with education?"

"I'm glad you asked that question, Andrea!" said Ms. Beard. "Each teacher is going to sing a song about the thing they teach. Let's start with your art teacher . . . Ms. Hannah!"

Everybody cheered when Ms. Hannah

went over to the microphone with a guitar.

"In art," she said, "sometimes we use tools to build sculptures. So I'd like to sing a song called 'If I Had a Hammer.'"

Ugh! I knew that song. It's about a guy who wants a hammer. He sings that if he had a hammer, he would hammer a bunch of stuff all over the world. If that's not dumb, I don't know what is.

Ms. Hannah sang the hammer song; and

when she was done, everybody clapped.

"Now let's see what our judges think," said Ms. Beard. "Andrea, did you like Ms. Hannah's song?"

"I thought it was lovely," said Andrea. "I give Mrs. Yonkers a ten."

Andrea held up a Ping-Pong paddle with a *10* on it, and everybody cheered.

"A perfect score!" said Ms. Beard. "A.J., how do *you* rate Ms. Hannah?"

"I give her a three," I said, holding up my paddle. "That song makes no sense at all. If she wants a hammer so badly, why doesn't she just go to a hardware store and buy one? Hammers don't cost that much."

"The song isn't about hammers, dumbhead!" Andrea said, rolling her eyes. "It's about peace."*

"What do *you* think, Ryan?" asked Ms. Beard.

"I give Ms. Hannah a six," said Ryan. "She said that if she had a hammer she would hammer in the morning. But I don't think she should hammer in the evening too. In the dark, she might hammer her thumb and hurt herself."

"Good point, Ryan," said Ms. Beard.

---

* If she wants peace, she should stop hammering all the time.

"Yeah, and hammering in the evening will disturb the neighbors," I added. "People are trying to sleep at night. They don't want to hear a bunch of hammering."

"Well said, A.J.!" said Ms. Beard. "That's nineteen points for Ms. Hannah."

Everybody cheered.

After that, Miss Holly, our Spanish teacher, sang a song called *"La Bamba."* Mr. Docker, our science teacher, sang a song called "She Blinded Me with Science." Mrs. Roopy, our librarian, sang a song about the Dewey decimal system. Miss Laney, our speech teacher, sang a song about the rain in Spain falling mainly on the plain. It made no sense at all. Who cares where it rains? Mr. Loring, our music teacher, sang a song called "Brown Sugar." That was weird. Why would anybody make a song about sugar?

After that came our computer teacher, Mrs. Yonkers.

"I'd like to sing a song about pork sausages," she said. "I borrowed the tune of 'Home on the Range.' It goes like this. . . ."

"Oh give me some pork
with a knife and a fork,
and potatoes that have been French
   fried.
It makes a great lunch,
and I'll eat a whole bunch
with a plateful of beans on the side.
Porky's pork sausages.
I'd rather eat them than play.
And when I am done,
I'll take one on a bun
To bring home and eat the next day."

"What do you think, judges?" asked Ms. Beard.

"That was *wonderful*!" said Andrea, who thinks that everything grown-ups do is wonderful. "I give it a ten."

"That was *terrible*!" I said. "Deaf people all over the world are grateful right now that they didn't have to hear that."

"What did that have to do with computers?" asked Ryan.

After the twelve teachers had sung a song, the phone lines were opened up, and people all over America had the chance to vote for their favorite. We had to wait a long time while the votes were being counted. Finally, Ms. Beard came out to announce the results.

"The people have spoken," she said. "Eleven of our teachers will move on to the next round. One of you must leave. But before I say who that teacher is, tell me, A.J., what do you think of pork sausages?"

"I give 'em a ten!" I said, holding up my paddle. "I love 'em!"

"You heard it here, folks!" said Ms. Beard.

"The judges agree that pork sausages are *great*! Now it's time to reveal which of our teachers got the least votes and will have to leave. That teacher is . . . Mrs. Roopy."

"Awwwwwwwwwww."

Mrs. Roopy walked off the stage, her head hanging.

One teacher eliminated, ten to go.

Dancing with the Teachers

When we got to the all-purpose room the next morning, there was a big banner across the stage . . .

DANCING WITH THE TEACHERS

The cameras started rolling right away, and Ms. Beard leaped up on the stage.

"Yesterday we saw how well the teachers

49

of Ella Mentry School could sing," she said. "Today we're going to see how well they dance!"

There were four pairs of dancers—two teams of Moosketeers and two teams of Hot Dog Heads. Ms. Beard announced that one of the couples would be eliminated. Andrea, Ryan, and I were called up to be the judges again.

"Our first couple will be Mr. Loring and Miss Holly of the Mooseketeers," said Ms. Beard. "They will be dancing the cha-cha."*

"I don't really know how to cha-cha," said Mr. Loring.

---

*Cha-cha? What kind of name is that for a dance?

"Me neither," said Miss Holly.

"Terrific!" shouted Ms. Beard. "Start the music!"

Some weird cha-cha music started playing.

Did you ever see a teacher dance? It's hilarious. You don't believe me? Ask your teacher to get up and dance, right now. It will be hysterical. I guarantee it.

Anyway, Miss Holly is really tall, and Mr. Loring is really short. They were stumbling all over and stepping on each other's feet while they tried to cha-cha. Ryan and I had to do all we could not to fall out of our seats laughing. I was afraid I was going to pee in my pants.

When it was over, everybody clapped and pretended that Mr. Loring and Miss Holly were good dancers.

"I give them a ten!" said Andrea, holding up her Ping-Pong paddle.

"I give them a one," I said. "They dance like a pair of water buffalo fighting over a piece of meat."

"I give them a two for effort," said Ryan.

"Okay! That's thirteen points," said Ms. Beard. "Let's bring on our next couple, Mr. Docker and Ms. Coco of the Hot Dog Heads."

Everybody cheered. They had to do a dance called the fox-trot. It didn't look like foxes trotting. It looked more like a

bad three-legged race. It was embarrass-ing just to watch. They weren't quite as awful as Mr. Loring and Miss Holly, but it was still the funniest thing in the history of the world. We gave them sixteen points, with ten of them from Andrea, of course.

"Next up, Mr. Granite and Miss Laney!" said Ms. Beard. "They will dance the tango."

I don't know what "tango" means, but it sure didn't look like dancing. It looked like Mr. Granite and Miss Laney were trying to stamp out cockroaches. We gave them twenty points.

The last dance team was Mr. Macky and Ms. Hannah. They had to do some dance called the rumba, and they were actually pretty good. Well, they were good for *teachers*, anyway. They got a nice round of applause, and twenty-five points.

Finally—and thankfully—Dancing with the Teachers was over. Ms. Beard added up the scores.

"If you ask me, *all* of these teachers are winners," she announced, "but two of you must be eliminated today. I'm sorry, but . . . Miss Holly and Mr. Loring will have to go home."

Three teachers eliminated, eight to go.

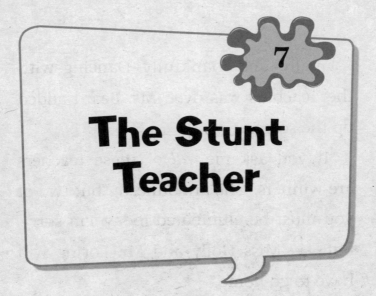

The Stunt Teacher

We were told to go back to class until the end of the day. Mr. Granite was happy about that. He said we could finally get some work done.

"Today we're going to talk about—"

But he didn't get the chance to finish his sentence, because you'll never believe who came running into the door at that moment.

Nobody! Why would you want to run into a door? That would hurt. But you'll never believe who came running into the *doorway*.

It was Ms. Beard, and a camera crew!

"Granite, baby!" she said, throwing her arm around Mr. Granite's shoulder. "I felt bad about what happened when we filmed you in class. I wanted to give you another chance to be a star."

"Uh . . . okay," said Mr. Granite.

All the lights and cameras were set up, and Ms. Beard yelled, "ACTION!"

"Today we're going to talk about

fractions," Mr. Granite told us. "A fraction is a number that expresses part of a group. The number above the line is called the numerator. The number below the line is called the—"

"Cut!" Ms. Beard yelled. "Granite, baby, you're putting everybody to sleep with that fraction mumbo jumbo. Try it again, and this time put a little pizzazz into it, will ya?"

"Uh . . . okay. I'll try."

"ACTION!"

"If two fractions have the same denominator," said Mr. Granite, "their sum is the sum of the numerators over the denomina—"

"Cut!" hollered Ms. Beard. "Bring in the

stunt teacher!"

"What?" shouted Mr. Granite. "Stunt teacher?"

"I'm sorry, Granite, baby, but this just isn't working out," said Ms. Beard. "I gotta bring in somebody who can grab viewers by the eyeballs."

"You can't do that!" protested Mr. Granite. "I spent years learning how to teach math."

"Chill, baby. It's temporary," said Ms. Beard. "Where's my stunt teacher? Where's Mr. Brown?"

Suddenly, a guy came walking into the class—on his hands. He did a somersault and a cartwheel and jumped up onto Mr. Granite's desk. He had a big red nose and orange hair sticking out on both sides.

"Hi, boys and girls!" he said in a funny voice, honking his nose.

"Mr. Brown is a clown!" I shouted.

"You can call me Brownie the Clownie!"

Mr. Granite stood there staring with his mouth open. Brownie skipped

out of the room and came back with a plate full of pies.

"Fractions are fun, kids!" he said. "If I cut this banana cream pie into eight slices and I eat one of them, how much of the pie did I eat?"

"One-eighth!" yelled Alexia, who is really good in math.

"Right!" said Brownie. "And if I were to take *two* slices of the pie and throw them at your teacher, how much of the pie would I throw?"

"One-fourth!" shouted Alexia. "Two-eighths is the same as one-fourth."

"Right!" shouted Brownie. Then he picked up two pieces of pie and threw them at Mr. Granite. They hit him right in the head. Banana cream was dribbling down his face.

Mr. Granite looked like he was going to *explode*. I had never seen him so mad.

"What if I took a *whole* pie," Mr. Granite shouted, "and shoved it in your clownie face?"

Mr. Granite picked up one of the pies and pushed it into Brownie's face. It was cool!

Then Brownie picked up another pie and threw it at Mr. Granite. But he ducked, and the pie hit Emily in the face instead. She was on the floor, freaking out. Then she went running out of the room. What a crybaby.

"Food fight!" we all hollered.

Mr. Granite and Brownie the Clown were furiously grabbing hunks of pie and throwing them at each other! Gobs of banana cream were flying all over the classroom!

When they ran out of pies to throw, Brownie the Clown and Mr. Granite started wrestling on the floor. It was a real Kodak moment.

Andrea pulled Ms. Beard off to the side.

"I really don't think this is going to help anybody learn about fractions," Andrea told her.

"Who cares?" replied Ms. Beard. "It makes great TV! The ratings will go through the roof!"

Free for All

When we got to school the next day, everybody was told to go around to the playground. And you'll never believe in a million hundred years what was back there.

A giant swimming pool! And it was filled with mud!

"Welcome to *The Real Teachers of Ella Mentry School*!" Ms. Beard said into the camera. "We know the teachers here are great singers and dancers. Today we're going to see if they're any good at mud wrestling!"

"Yay!" everybody went except for Andrea, who rolled her eyes and said it looked disgusting.

The teachers were standing at the edge of the pool wearing bikinis. It was hilarious. Believe me, Mr. Docker does *not* look good in a bikini.

"When I blow my whistle, all the teachers will jump into the pool," said Ms. Beard. "The first four teachers who climb out will advance to the next round. The others will be eliminated. Is everybody ready?"

"This is gonna be cool!" I said to Michael.

"What are we going to learn from *this*?" asked Andrea. "It doesn't sound very educational to me."

"Oh, that's where you're wrong," said Ms. Beard. "While the teachers are mud wrestling, they also have to recite multiplication tables! On your mark . . . get set . . . GO!"

Ms. Beard blew her whistle. The teachers jumped into the pool. We all started yelling and screaming.

As soon as Miss Small landed in the mud, she started to climb out of the pool, but Mr. Macky grabbed her before she reached the edge and threw her into the middle. She was completely covered in mud. Then Mr. Macky tried to climb out of the pool, but Miss Laney grabbed his leg, and he fell face-first into the mud. He made a big *splat*.

"Don't forget about your times tables!" shouted Ms. Beard.

"One times three is three," yelled Ms. Leakey as she grabbed Ms. Coco and put her in a headlock.

"Two times three is six," yelled Mr. Granite as he dived on top of Mrs. Yonkers.

Mud was flying *everywhere*! Every time one of the teachers tried to climb out of the pool, one of the other teachers would pull them back into the mud. It was getting hard to tell who was who, because all

the teachers were brown and slimy and
slippery.

"Three times three is nine," yelled Ms.

Hannah as she got hit with a mud pie in the face.

"Four times three is twelve," yelled Miss Laney as she belly flopped into the muck.

"Wow, these teachers are great wrestlers!" shouted Ms. Beard. "And they really know their math!"

Finally, Ms. Leakey and Mr. Macky teamed up to dunk Ms. Coco, and they managed to climb out of the pool together.

"Eat mud, you Hot Dog Heads!" shouted Mr. Macky. "The Mooseketeers rule the pool!"

While they were celebrating, Mr. Granite and Miss Small climbed out of the other end of the pool together. Ms. Beard blew her whistle to signal that the game was over.

"Okay!" she shouted. "The winners are Ms. Leakey and Mr. Macky of the Moosketeers, and Miss Small and Mr. Granite of the Hot Dog Heads. The other teachers are eliminated. Let's give *all* our teacher wrestlers a big round of applause!"

We all cheered and whistled and clapped in a circle. Mr. Docker, Ms. Coco, Miss Laney, Ms. Hannah, and Mrs. Yonkers slowly climbed out of the pool covered from head to toe with yucky mud. They looked like a bunch of chocolate Easter bunnies.

We're Outta Here

When we got to school the next day, Ms. Beard was all excited. She told us that every night, millions more people were tuning in to watch *The Real Teachers of Ella Mentry School* on TV. Everybody wanted to see who was going to be the winner.

"The ratings are through the roof!" she said.

There were just four teachers left: Mr. Macky and Ms. Leakey of the Mooseketeers, and Miss Small and Mr. Granite of the Hot Dog Heads. After all that singing, dancing, and mud wrestling, they were worn-out, tired, and maybe even a little cranky.

"Okay!" Ms. Beard announced to the camera. "Today our teachers are going to bake cakes. The teacher who bakes the best cake—"

She didn't get the chance to finish her sentence.

"That's dumb!" yelled Miss Small. "I

don't want to bake a cake."

"Me neither," said Mr. Macky.

"I don't know the first thing about baking a cake," said Ms. Leakey.

"This is ridiculous," said Mr. Granite. "What could baking cakes possibly have to do with education?"

"Nothing," replied Ms. Beard. "But our research shows that people like to watch other people bake cakes on TV."

"Well, we're not doing it!" announced Mr. Granite.

"Yeah!" said Miss Small. "If I have to bake a cake, I'm outta here."

"Me too!" said Mr. Granite. "Find us something else to do."

"Uh . . . okay," said Ms. Beard. "Today our teachers are going to eat bugs. The teacher who eats the most bugs—"

"I'm not eating bugs!" yelled Mr. Macky. He was really mad.

"But our research shows that next to

baking cakes, the one thing people like to watch most on TV is other people eating bugs," said Ms. Beard.

"I don't care what your research shows," shouted Mr. Macky. "I'm not eating bugs. And by the way, that's my final answer."

"I've had enough of reality TV," said Mr. Granite. "I quit."

"What if we had a tug-of-war?" suggested Ms. Beard. "And the team that loses falls into a pit filled with Porky's pork sausages?"

"No!" all four teachers replied.

"Look," Mr. Macky said, "we're not falling into any pits. We're not going to eat any bugs. And we're not going to bake cakes or wrestle in mud anymore. We're sick of your dumb games, so we're leaving the show."

"Don't you care about winning the—"

"No!"

The four teachers got up to leave.

"Wait!" shouted Ms. Beard, stopping them. "Okay, I get it. I won't make you bake cakes or eat bugs or fall into pits filled with pork sausages. But if you stay, I'll donate *another* million dollars to the school."

They stopped.

"What's the catch?" asked Miss Small.

"You will have to do the most challenging, frightening, and humiliating thing anyone has ever done on a TV show," said Ms. Beard.

"What?" asked the teachers.

And you'll never believe in a million hundred years what the teachers would have to do.

I'm not gonna tell you.

Okay, okay, I'll tell you. But you have to read the next chapter.*

---

*So na-nah-nah boo-boo on you.

Very Funny

"You have to tell jokes," announced Ms. Beard.

"Jokes?"

"Oh, that's no big deal," said Ms. Leakey. "I know lots of jokes."

"Me too," said Mr. Granite.

"Here are the rules," announced Ms. Beard. "The four of you can tell three jokes each. Then we'll open up the phone lines, and viewers will vote for the funniest teacher. Two of you will advance to the next round, and two of you will go home. Got it? Let's get cracking. Joke cracking, that is!"

All the lights went out except for a spotlight on the microphone. Mr. Granite stepped up to it.

"What kind of a bone will a dog never eat?" asked Mr. Granite.

"What kind?" we all shouted.

"A trombone!" said Mr. Granite.

He waited until the chuckles died down

to tell his next joke.

"Who can shave twenty-five times a day and still have a beard?"

"Who?" we all shouted.

"A barber!" said Mr. Granite. "Did you hear about the fire at the circus?"

"No," we all shouted.

"It was in tents," said Mr. Granite.

We gave Mr. Granite a standing ovation. He bowed, and Ms. Leakey stepped up to the microphone.

"Have you heard about the new

corduroy pillows?" she asked. "They're making headlines! But seriously, folks, do you know what Mary is short for?"

"What?" we all shouted.

"She's got no legs," said Ms. Leakey. "Hey, why was Jon walking backward on the first day of school?"

"Why?" we all shouted.

"It was back-to-school time," said Ms. Leakey. "Thank you. You've been a wonderful audience."

"That was terrific!" said Ms. Beard over the applause. "Let's bring out our next comedian."

Mr. Macky stepped up to the microphone.

"Do you kids know what the Atlantic and Pacific Oceans said to each other?" he asked.

"What?" we all shouted.

"Nothing," said Mr. Macky. "They just waved. Hey, why do gorillas have big nostrils?"

"Why?" we all shouted.

"Because gorillas have big fingers," said Mr. Macky. "Say, how are a chicken and a grape alike?"

"How?" we all shouted.

"They're both purple," said Mr. Macky, "except for the chicken."

"Good one!" said Ms. Beard. "And last but not least, how about a round of applause for your gym teacher, Miss Small!"

Miss Small stepped up to the microphone.

"What has four legs, is big, green, fuzzy, and if it fell out of a tree would kill you?" she asked.

"What?" we all shouted.

"A pool table," said Miss Small. "Do you

kids know why a bicycle can't stand up by itself?"

"Why?" we all shouted.

"It's two tired," said Miss Small. "Hey, what's Irish and sits out in the backyard?"

"What?" we all shouted.

"Patio furniture."

The teachers weren't all that funny, but we laughed anyway, because it's funny watching teachers tell jokes. Just like it's funny watching teachers sing, dance, and mud wrestle.

Actually, watching teachers do anything besides teach is funny.

Ms. Beard announced that the phone lines were open, and millions of hundreds of people started calling in. We had to sit and wait forever while the votes were counted. Then we had to sit through another commercial for Porky's pork sausages.

"After this there will only be two teachers left," Andrea said to me. "Isn't this exciting, Arlo?"

"No," I replied.

Actually, it was *really* exciting. But any time Andrea says anything, I always say the opposite thing. That's the first rule of being me.

Finally, the phone lines were closed. Ms. Beard stepped up to the microphone with a piece of paper.

"I have the results," she said. "America has spoken. "Our last two teachers are . . . Mr. Granite and Ms. Leakey!"

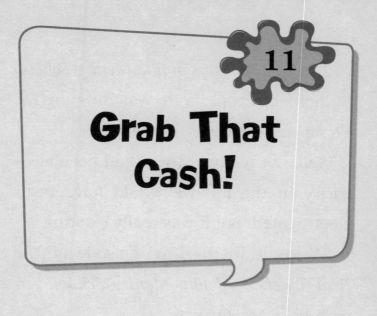

11

Grab That Cash!

So after a week of competition, there were only two teachers left: Mr. Granite of the Hot Dog Heads and Ms. Leakey of the Mooseketeers.

The next night we all gathered in the all-purpose room for the final live episode of *The Real Teachers of Ella Mentry School*. Millions of people were watching on TV. There was electricity in the air.

Well, not really. If there had been electricity in the air, we would have been electrocuted. But it was really exciting.

"Welcome to the final episode of *The Real Teachers of Ella Mentry School*! I'm your host, Ms. Beard."

Everybody clapped and stomped their feet. Some kids were holding up signs like **MS. LEAKEY IS FREAKY!** and **MR. GRANITE IS FROM ANOTHER PLANET!**

"Go, Mr. Granite!" I shouted.

"You can do it, Ms. Leakey!" shouted somebody else.

Two big booths were wheeled out

onto the stage. They looked like the old-fashioned phone booths they had before everybody used cell phones.

The doors were opened. Mr. Granite and Ms. Leakey each got into a booth. There were microphones, so we could hear what they said.

"Are you two nervous?" asked Ms. Beard.

"A little, yes," said Mr. Granite.

"Not me!" said Ms. Leakey. "I'm ready for anything."

"Great!" said Ms. Beard. "This game is simple. We're going to open the top of both booths and drop hundreds of dollar bills on you. When I say go, start grabbing the bills. Whoever grabs the most money in five minutes will be the winner of *The Real Teachers of Ella Mentry School.*"

"*Yayyyyyyyyyyyyyyyyy!*"

"That doesn't look so hard," I whispered to Alexia, who was sitting next to me.

Two guys climbed up on ladders and opened the tops of the booths. Then they dumped garbage cans full of dollar bills into them.

"Can we get started?" asked Mr. Granite.

"Not yet," said Ms. Beard. "Okay, guys, drop the glue!"

Glue?

The guys on the ladders took hoses and pointed them down into the booths. Then they turned the hoses on and squirted thick globs of glue all over Mr. Granite and Ms. Leakey until they were completely covered.

Yuck! Disgusting!

"Can we get started *now*?" asked Ms. Leakey.

"Not yet," said Ms. Beard. "Okay, guys, turn on the fans!"

Fans?

There must have been fans in the bottom of the booths, because suddenly there was a loud whooshing sound, and the dollar bills started swirling all over the place.

"Okay, *now* you can get started!" shouted Ms. Beard. "Go! Go! Go! Grab that cash!"

Mr. Granite and Ms. Leakey started flailing around, trying to snatch the money that was flying all over the

booths. Some of the bills stuck to their clothes. Some of it stuck to their faces. Mr. Granite was stuffing dollar bills into his pockets. Ms. Leakey was stuffing them down her shirt.

"This doesn't seem very educational to me," said Andrea.

But it *was* hilarious. And we got to see it live and in person. You should have been there!

"GO! GO! GO!" we all chanted. "GRAB THAT CASH!"

After five minutes, a buzzer sounded. The fans were turned off, and the money floated down to the bottom. Ms. Leakey and Mr. Granite staggered out of the booths like they were drunk. There was money and glue stuck all over them. Everybody clapped.

"That was *great*!" Ms. Beard said, sticking the microphone into their faces. "How do you feel?"

"Fuffrumprugrym," said Mr. Granite. His mouth was full of dollar bills, so he couldn't talk very well.

The bills were peeled off and collected so they could be counted to find out who was the winner. It took a long time. We had to sit through a bunch of commercials for Porky's pork sausages. But everyone was excited. We were on pins and needles.

Well, not really. We were sitting on

chairs. If we were on pins and needles, it would have hurt.*

Finally, Ms. Beard came out with an envelope in her hand. A hush fell over the all-purpose room.

"Well," she said as she tore open the envelope, "this is the moment you've been waiting for, America! We tallied up all the money. Mr. Granite grabbed two hundred and fifty-six dollars!"

"Yay!" all the kids in my class shouted.

". . . and Ms. Leakey grabbed three hundred and twenty-four dollars!" shouted Ms. Beard. "The winner of *The Real Teachers of Ella Mentry School* is Ms. Leakey!"

---

*But it probably wouldn't have hurt as much as it would if there was electricity in the air.

Everybody started yelling and screaming and clapping and stomping and freaking out. About a million hundred balloons fell from the ceiling.

Ms. Leakey and Mr. Granite hugged each other. They had a hard time separating after that because they were covered with glue. Everybody laughed.

"Mr. Granite, you get to keep all the cash you grabbed," said Ms. Beard. "And Ms. Leakey, you not only get to keep your cash, but you also win an all-expenses-paid vacation to anywhere in the world! How do you feel?"

"I don't know what to say," said Ms. Leakey as she tried to wipe the tears of joy and glue off her face.

"Don't forget, you also win a year's supply of Porky's pork sausages," said Ms. Beard

"I *love* pork sausages!" shouted Ms. Leakey.

Well, that's pretty much what happened. *The Real Teachers of Ella Mentry School*

was a big hit on TV. Ms. Beard bought lots of computers, pencils, notebooks, and toilet paper for our school. After it was all over, we found out that Ms. Beard owned the Porky's Pork Sausage Company.

Maybe Ms. Leakey will share her pork sausages with us. Maybe Ms. Beard will stop calling Mr. Klutz Chickie Baby. Maybe they'll make a TV show about Emily's toenails. Maybe that guy will go to a hardware store and buy a hammer instead of just singing about it all the time. Maybe the teachers will learn how to cha-cha. Maybe Brownie the Clownie will teach us more about fractions. Maybe we'll get to mud wrestle during fizz ed class. Maybe they'll take the electricity out of the air before somebody gets hurt. Maybe Mr. Granite will be able to finish a lesson for once.

But it won't be easy!

12

I Hate When That Happens

Oh, I forgot to tell you something.

After *The Real Teachers of Ella Mentry School* was on TV, we were all celebrities. Big sacks full of fan mail started arriving at my house. Reporters wanted to interview me. People began asking me for autographs. It was cool.

Well, it was cool in the *beginning* anyway. After a while it got to be annoying. Now I can barely go outside without being chased down the street by my fans.

You don't believe me? Watch this. I'm going to step outside for a minute.

"Look! It's him!"

"*It's A.J. from* The Real Teachers of Ella Mentry School*!*"

"*I love him!*"

Uh-oh. This was a big mistake.

"*Can I have your autograph, A.J.?*"

"*He's cuter than Justin Bieber!*"

"*A.J., I want to marry you!*"

"I want a lock of his hair!"

"Get him!"

Oh no! I've got to make a run for it!

They're chasing me down the street like wild dogs!

I'm out of breath.

What's that noise?

It's up in the sky!

It sounds like . . . oh *no*!

There's a helicopter following me!

It's from the TV news!

They're pointing big searchlights at me!

It's getting lower!

What am I gonna do?

Help! The helicopter is landing on my *head*!